Zamboni's Bath

written by
Vicki Scott Burns

illustrated by
Linda Pierce

KAEDEN ❤ BOOKS

Title: Zamboni's Bath
Copyright © 2007 Kaeden Corporation
Author: Vicki Scott Burns
Illustrator: Linda Pierce

ISBN: 978-1-57874-339-1

Published by:
Kaeden Corporation
P.O. Box 16190
Rocky River, Ohio 44116
1-800-890-7323
www.kaeden.com

Printed in Canada

10 9 8 7 6 5 4 3 2 1

Contents

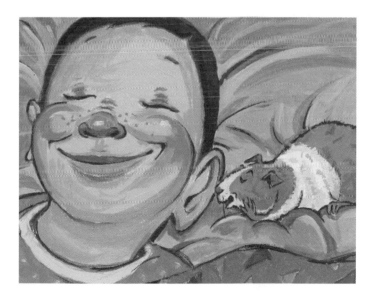

—1—

The Great Escape

His name is Zamboni. Billy calls him Zam for short. Zam is the coolest guinea pig in the whole world! His favorite thing to do is sleep on Billy's pillow. Billy takes Zam to bed with him every night. Zam curls up into a tight, furry ball next to Billy's head.

Zam likes to watch Billy's face as he dreams. Billy's mouth stretches into a smile from ear to ear and his nose scrunches up into a freckled ball. Billy always smiles in his sleep as Zam chatters into his ear.

Today began like every other day. Billy moaned as his alarm clock announced the morning's arrival. He nudged Zam off his shoulder and rolled out of bed.

After Billy put on his clothes, he walked over to the bed and scooped Zam into his hands. "Morning, Zam," he mumbled as he rubbed Zam's ears.

Zam closed his eyes and purred. Billy giggled as he gently set Zam down in his cage. Billy ran downstairs for breakfast.

Billy didn't know that Zam could get out of his cage. As soon as Billy left the room, Zam pushed his food dish to the front of the cage. He hopped up onto the edge of the dish and stood on his tiny hind feet. With his front legs stretched up toward the ceiling, he mustered all of his guinea pig strength. He scrunched up his nose, held his breath and jumped with all his might. He felt himself leaping, then flying, and then, freedom!

He landed with a thud next to Billy's backpack. He quickly scurried through the open zipper.

A few minutes later, Billy bounded into his room and grabbed the backpack. He plunked his lunchbox next to Zam and closed the zipper.

—2—

Zam's First Day of School

When they got to school, Billy hung his backpack on the back of his chair. He unzipped the backpack and grabbed his book. He left the zipper open.

Zam listened to the sounds of the classroom. He rummaged through Billy's stuff: a pair of gloves, his hockey cards, and his lunchbox.

Zam was hungrily sniffing the lunchbox when Billy stood up and knocked his backpack onto the floor. Then Zam spied the open zipper.

Zam crept out of the backpack. His eyes scanned the classroom. There were a million guinea-pig-sized nooks and crannies, and there were crumbs everywhere!

Zam wasted no time. He scurried across the floor, dodging second-grade-sized feet as he hungrily snatched the crumbs.

Zam climbed onto a shelf packed with stuffed animals. He sniffed each one as he made his way across the shelf. He hopped onto the floor and headed towards the ball bin.

Suddenly, a very loud bell rang and kids were grabbing their coats and lunches. Stomping feet surrounded him!

A fluffy, purple sweatshirt was on the floor right in front of him. Zam spied an empty pocket. He tiptoed across the sweatshirt and stuck his head into the pocket. He squiggled, wiggled and squirmed like a worm. He made it into the pocket just as the sweatshirt's owner picked it up off the floor.

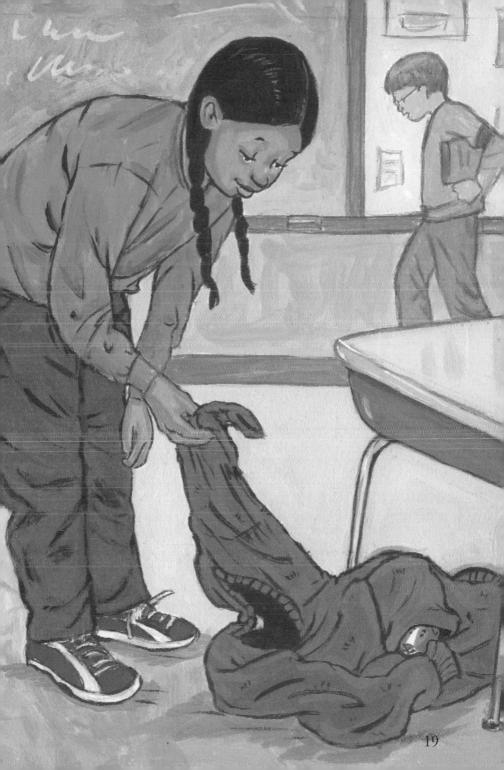

—3—

Zam's Unexpected Bath

As they entered the cafeteria, Zam smelled something scrumptious. The girl plopped her fluffy, purple sweatshirt onto the counter. Zam quickly scooted out of the pocket and hid behind a stack of trays.

Before long, Zam just had to follow his nose. He scurried along the counter to a tray full of burgers. He was drooling with anticipation!

As Zam sank his teeth into the juiciest of burgers, the cook let out the scariest of screams! Zam froze in his tracks. The cook screamed, "Rat! Rat! There's a rat!"

Zam kept on nibbling. The cook ran towards him flailing a metal spatula. That's when Zam realized that she was aiming for him! He stole another nibble from the burger then ran as quickly as his stubby legs would allow.

The cook kept smacking the spatula on the counters, the kids were screaming, and everyone was running in circles.

In all of the chaos, no one saw Zam scurry away. As he wobbled along the counter, he looked back over his shoulder to make sure that he wasn't being followed.

Suddenly, his front paws hit a slippery puddle and he slid face first into a sink full of soapy water.

Zam frantically paddled his four paws while he tried to hold his nose above the water. The more he paddled, the bubblier the water became.

Soon, bubbles were covering his entire head! He paddled and paddled and paddled. Zam was sure he would drown.

Once again, he mustered all of his guinea pig strength. He took a deep breath and paddled as mightily as he could.

That's when Zam realized that he was running on something. His feet were touching the bottom of the sink. The water was only a few inches deep!

Zam tried to climb out of the sink but he was too wet and slippery. His front paws couldn't grab onto the ledge.

He heard the commotion behind him as grown-ups continued to search for the cook's rat. Zam hid beneath the bubbles and walked around the sink, trying to find a better climbing spot.

His tiny claws banged into a pot. He climbed on top of the pot and then hopped onto the counter.

He shook off the bubbly water. He tried to run but his soapy feet slid across the counter. He closed his eyes, held his breath and waited for the crash.

Zam slid into something soft and cuddly. It was the fluffy, purple sweatshirt! He crammed himself back into the pocket and stayed very still.

Before long, the sweatshirt was plopped back onto the classroom floor. Zam backed out of the pocket and spotted Billy's red shoes across the room.

Zam had experienced enough adventures for one day. He scampered over to Billy's feet. The backpack's zipper was still open and Zam crawled right through it. He curled up in a dark corner and fell fast asleep.

—4—

Sweet Dreams

A few hours later, Billy dropped his backpack onto his bedroom floor right next to Zam's cage.

After Billy left the room, Zam crawled out of the backpack, quickly scurried up his water bottle and nestled back into his cage.

When Billy fell asleep that night, Zam curled up into a tight, furry ball next to Billy's head. Zam watched Billy's face as he dreamed.

Dreams are the special place where Zam can tell Billy about his adventures. Zam told Billy about his unexpected bath that day at school. Billy's mouth stretched into a smile and his nose scrunched up into a freckled ball as Zam chattered into his ear.